Eoin McLaughlin  Polly Dunbar

The Kiss

The Kiss

For Charlie and Sofia
E.M.

First published in the UK in 2023
First published in the US in 2023
by Faber and Faber Limited
The Bindery, 51 Hatton Garden, London EC1N 8HN
Text © Eoin McLaughlin, 2023 Illustrations © Polly Dunbar, 2023
Design by Faber
US HB ISBN 978–0–571–36188–5
PB ISBN 978–0–571–36189–2
All rights reserved.
Printed in Latvia
10 9 8 7 6 5 4 3 2
The moral rights of Eoin McLaughlin and Polly Dunbar have been asserted.
A CIP record for this book is available from the British Library.

Faber has published children's books since 1929. T. S. Eliot's *Old Possum's Book of Practical Cats* and Ted Hughes' *The Iron Man* were amongst the first. Our catalogue at the time said that 'it is by reading such books that children learn the difference between the shoddy and the genuine'. We still believe in the power of reading to transform children's lives. All our books are chosen with the express intention of growing a love of reading, a thirst for knowledge and to cultivate empathy. We pride ourselves on responsible editing. Last but not least, we believe in kind and inclusive books in which all children feel represented and important.

Tiger was feeling sleepy.
As sleepy as sleepy can be.

yaaaawn

So sleepy, only one thing could help.

"I really must go to bed," said Tiger.
"Might you give me a kiss goodnight?"

"I'm just in the middle of nibbling something," said Mouse. "And then I'm going to climb into my hole."

"I'm in my hole now."

"It's very much past my bedtime. Will somebody give me the tiniest kiss goodnight?"

"We're asleep already," said the monkeys.

"Honestly, we are."

"I'm ever so sleepy," said Tiger.
"Please may I have a kiss goodnight?"

"No one will kiss me goodnight.
Nobody will tuck me in.
I shall never get to sleep.
I shall always be awake."

"I wish I could give you a kiss," said Moon,
"but look, here comes . . .

"There you are!" said Tiger's daddy.
"It's time for bed, little one.
Now, where's my . . .

"kiss!"

„Kiss!"

"There you are!" said Crocodile's mummy.
"It's time for bed, little one.
Now, where's my . . .

"Mummy!"

"I wish I could give you a kiss," said Moon,
"but look, here comes . . .

"No one will kiss me goodnight.
Nobody will tuck me in.
I shall never get to sleep.
I shall always be awake."

Kiss,
smooch,
mwwaaaah!

"We only kiss each other," said the toucans. "We hope you understand."

"Will *anyone* give me a kiss goodnight?"

"A very deep bath."

"Please," said Crocodile.
"I need a goodnight kiss."

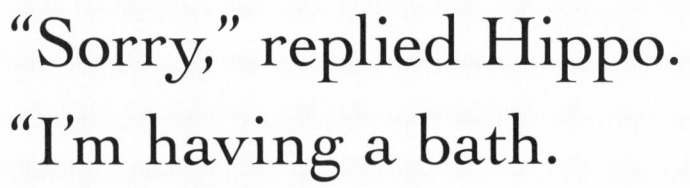

"Sorry," replied Hippo.
"I'm having a bath.

"I don't see any chameleon."

"Chameleon?" said Chameleon.

"Hello, Chameleon," said Crocodile.
"Might I trouble you for a kiss goodnight?"

So sleepy, only one thing could help.

Crocodile was feeling sleepy.
As sleepy as sleepy can be.

Eoin McLaughlin ♥ Polly Dunbar

The Kiss

The Roar

Eoin McLaughlin ❧ Polly Dunbar

Winter had been long...

The Longer the Wait,
the Bigger the Hug

Eoin McLaughlin ❧ Polly Dunbar

While We
Can't Hug

Eoin McLaughlin ❧ Polly Dunbar

The Hug

Eoin McLaughlin ❧ Polly Dunbar

For Suzy, Ron and little Jimmy x
P.D.

The Kiss